GOD'S SONG...

...and How We Sing It

GOD'S SONG...

...and How We Sing It

Sister Ave Clark, O.P.

Sister Ave Clark, O.P.
Heart to Heart Ministry
718-428-2471
Pearlbud7@aol.com
www.h2h.nyc

Rachel Prayer Hour: post abortion syndrome

Elizabeth Ministry: for parents who lost a child

Caring Hearts: for people with PTSD

ROSES: for survivors of abuse/domestic violence

ACOA: for adult children of alcoholics

Caritas: for family with children/adult with a disability

Hearts Afire: domestic violence (individual)

Lights in the Darkness: persons seeking healing from depression

Bereavement Sessions: From the Heart (individual)

Spiritual Direction: Open Your Heart (individual)

Pastoral Prayer-line: A Listening Heart

Podcast Nun: Everyday Graces

Podcast Nun 2: Heart Conversations

Heart to Heart Prayer Chats: Across the Country

Only the wings of love and compassion
can lift and carry us

God's Song is a Prayer
Heart to Heart
Full of Grace
with a wonderful holy light
It is filled with love
echoing a beautiful, harmonious tone
of faithfulness into
all hearts in the world…
where peace and justice
and kindness and caring
bless everyone…
Keeping each one of us safe and
guiding us "together" to joyously choose
to become more of God's "prayerful" song
here on earth's "holy" adventure.

IN MEMORY
A piece of my heart holds their song

Filomena (Fanny) Aloi
Father Coleman Costello
Sister Rosemary Hickey, O.P.
Norma Mosia
Henry Palmer

Good People of Faith...who lived their ordinary lives with courage and a song in their hearts of wonderful kindness

"I thank my God whenever I think of you"
(Philippians 1:3)

TABLE OF CONTENTS

Special Message: Imagine singing with God! I hope
you will as you read and reflect on the thoughts in
this book. Perhaps you will find yourself humming
as you turn each page. You might even discover
new songs to sing with and about God's love in
your life.

Personal Reflections: are sprinkled throughout the book.
Enjoy sharing your creative thoughts about God's
Songs and how you courageously and lovingly dare
to live them to make the world a better place for all
people to live. You might even write a verse of a
new song that is in your heart.

Chapters: the chapters in this book will not be titled or
given a page number in the content. The author
invites you to open to a page anywhere and reflect
on God's Song in your life. You might just be
humming or singing a lyric of God's Song on every
page.

DEDICATION

 Sometimes you meet people in life that
live God's Song in ordinary
and extraordinary ways.

Roseann Maggio

A home care nurse who provides a great ministry of comfort and care to homebound persons. This caring heart of Roseann spills over into her daily encounters, bringing a smile of God's Song everywhere she goes.

Sister Mary Pat Neylon, O.P.

An Amityville Dominican Sister, who has a song in her heart sprinkled with God's Song of Faithfulness. Anyone who meets Sister Mary Pat will feel the Song of God's kindness and tenderness. Sister Mary Pat sings a song of God's holy encouragement and hope to all people.

Octavia Willis

Octavia's song is one of humility and simplicity along with a wonderful and cheerful disposition. Octavia sings God's Song of trust and faith lived and shared so that others can feel God's presence in their encounters with her. Octavia lives God's prayer song.

PROLOGUE

Music is life itself!
~~Louie Armstrong

Sister Ave Clark has done it again! This latest book in her series of personal life-reflections will open you to the heart of music, and deeply touch your mind, body, and spirit.

As the ancient philosopher Plato once wrote: "Music gives a soul to the universe, wings to the mind, flight to the imagination and life to everything". As you enter into the melodies of this book, you will become more keenly aware of the power of music to touch the soul. Whether its jazz, gospel, classical, contemporary or chant, each in its own way moves the spirit to respond. What is your favorite genre, and how has it moved you to listen, ponder and respond?

Yes, we are called to respond, called to be God's song of love, each in our own unique way. For myself, I've been playing the flute and "making music" since I was nine years old. Whether in a marching band, orchestra, school, parish, hospital, or nursing home, it has been a privilege to share my gift of music celebrations of life: weddings, jubilees, baptisms, funerals, religious services, as well as comforting the sick and the dying. Now in my 85th year, I continue to play and realize that it has become a musical expression of my prayer and relationship with the Holy Mystery.

As you reflect on your own musical history, in what way do you sing God's song of love?

I now invite you to enjoy reading reflections on this universal language of music and allow it to speak to your soul. Together, as we enter deeply into the music of the universe, we can and will make the world a more compassionate, creative, and melodious place for all.

Sister Mary Anna Euring, O.P.
Amityville Dominican Sister

(I do not play a musical instrument, but I do appreciate greatly those who do...listening brings me to a peace-filled encounter with God's Song. I hope someday you all get to hear Sister Mary Anna play her flute...it sure comes from a heart with a beautiful song.)

"Sing to him, sing praise to the Lord,
tell of all his wonderful works"
(Psalm 105:1-2)

"Sing to the Lord, a new song"
(Psalm 96:1)

"...and with my song, I praise him with thanks-giving"
(Psalm 28:7)

"I will sing, O Lord, of your mercies, of your love forever"
(Psalm 89:1)

Your love, O God is my song
the Universe of stars, sun, moon, and planets

the clouds, rain and snow
the sun shining
day and night
the earth
water, land, plants, and
creatures

And we human beings praise
you, Lord
given a heart-spirit to love with
we sing a Song of Love
and God sings…

You are my Beloved.

AUTHOR'S NOTE

Music is a wonderful gift. It invites you into a space of holy reflection. Listening to music can soothe and comfort your spirit. It also can inspire you. Think of a song you like and why. You find yourself humming it. Music can change your mood. It can uplift your spirit.

When I taught students in my special education class to sing together, they would smile and say God loves our singing because we sing with many hearts. I smiled as we sang God's Songs with our own tunes. One of my students said, "bet God likes the way we sing" ...again I smiled and agreed.

No one should ever say I cannot sing or be told not to sing because they find it difficult to hold a tune. Just sing with all your heart. God gives us his melody of Love to share, and we do that in a variety of ways. We become co-creators of God's Song by sharing...

...peace and joy
...hope and encouragement
...kindness and compassion
...love and faithfulness

You and I have a marvelous mission to share as we hum God's Song into our daily life encounters. Together we create new verses to go with God's Song. God's Songs are all about being a good human being who cares about others.

Good Samaritan	Luke 10:29-37
Healing the Leper	Matthew 8:1-14
Dining with a Sinner	Luke 19:1-10
Showing Compassion	Luke 8:40-48
Forgiveness	Luke 22:47-52

Sing with all your heart as you read these Scripture passages. Let us take God's notes of peace and kindness and become them in our daily lives. Remember, everybody can sing God's Song!

GOD SONGS

Did you ever wonder why poets and composers write
        so many songs about the topic and theme of love?
They try to understand it, express it, reveal it.
If love is God, then God is love.
John Lennon of the Beatles said it is all you need.
The reggae group, Third World, said now that we found love
        what are we going to do with it?
And Todd Rundgren of the rock group Utopia said it is the
        answer
What are your questions?
Listen to the lyrics of his song of the same title
And when you feel afraid, love one another
When you've lost your way, love one another
When you're all alone, love one another
When you're far from home, love one another
When you're down and out, love one another
When all your hope's run out, love one another
When you need a friend, love one another
When you're near the end, love one another
We got to love, we got to love one another
Light of the world, you got to shine on me
Love is the answer
Shine on us all, set us free
Love is the answer
And maybe Bob Marley asked the most important question of
all…
                  Could you be Love?

 (James Palmaro, a gifted poet with heart words written
in prose. He himself is disabled with blindness and sees
the world through his faith-lived with great love.)

—

IMAGINE...God using a banjo, guitar, or a harmonica. There is a small light on the earth and as God sings the light gets brighter and brighter. His smile is now seen. It is a loving, gentle, and tender smile.

God looks out into the world of humanity as he sings...
...to every one of every age...everywhere
...to every yearning spirit
...to every human heart longing for peace

The song...
...is simple and profound
...direct and deeply honest
...full of wisdom and patience
...is unifying with justice
...has unconditional love and compassion
...is prophetic and divine

God's songs are challenging, they tell us to...
... "let go" of selfish self-serving ways
...ego-centered thoughts
...controlling actions
...negative thoughts
God's Songs are "truth-filled" ...VERITAS

"You shall know the truth, and truth shall set you free"
(John 8:32).

"I am the way, the truth, and the life"
(John 14:6)

Being human, limited and flawed, we humans very often fall short of singing in unison with God's Song. Let us not miss any opportunity, even an unwanted disruption to find new ways to sing God's Song in new, healthy, and wholesome ways and be transformed.

How do we do this?

Remember these 5 truths...
...We are never alone
...God is ever-present
...God's grace is sufficient
...We are called to love
...God makes all things new

> *"Behold~~I am making all things new"*
> (Revelations 21:5)

When we live God's Song...the earth and our hearts will be filled with light, love, and life-giving hope. Our little hums help us to deal better with the "unexpected" by making healthy choices that help us to handle stress in life better. These spiritual hums help us to reconnect our humanity with the message of God's Song.

The Holy Spirit gifts us with lyrics that include...
...holy courage
...amazing graces
...strength to carry our crosses
...blessings to be a faithful disciple

God's Songs don't always make us feel comfortable. Sometimes we humans try to adjust God's tune to fit our own self-centered way.

We have trouble forgiving once or even twice. God says forgive 70 times 7. God says "Come follow me" ...we sometimes say...not now God!

God's Songs have tunes that "free us" to choose to be his goodness in the world. This inner freedom is a sacred place where divine love energizes our hearts and spirits to respond in tune with God's harmonious ways.

We are called to not just listen to God's Songs but to let them become a life-giving lyric in our life that shares...
...mercy and justice
...peace and harmony
...kindness and charity
...respect and dignity
...forgiveness and reconciliation

How do you let God's Songs inspire" holy goodness" to be in your very human heart-peace melodies? How do you share the resonance of God's compassionate song in your daily life encounters?

"Sing and make music with your heart"
(Ephesians 5:19)

God sings of "blessings" that anoint the earth.
God prays in songs that draw us closer to his love.
(Matthew 6:5-15)

Pray the Our Father quietly...you can also sing it.

As you pray and praise the Lord in prayer you will with the Lord's love restore peace and harmony to the universe. God's Song is a spiritual way of connecting the holy into our daily life. In the silent faithfulness of prayer, we befriend the mystery of God's love.

Love is not idle.
(St. Catherine of Siena)

Can you imagine God singing?   I can!
What does his voice sound like?
What song is God singing to you?
What do you like about God's Song?

God's Songs take us on a pilgrimage
to discover a holy song in all
the facets of our life.

God's Song embraces every breath of life. His songs
help us...
...explore
...awaken
...create
...investigate
...search
...examine
...acknowledge
...interpret
...accept
...discover

God's Song offers...
...welcome
...hospitality
...friendship
...community
...gatherings
...encounters

God's Songs provide...
...a good experience
...a way of trust
...a holy commitment

God's Song gives us a "promise" that his fine
tune will remain with us...forever and ever.

We live God's Song simply by...

    ...breathing

    ...walking

    ...resting

    ...working

    ...sleeping

    ...playing

    ...cooking

    ...cleaning

    ...reading

All is...

    ...sacred

    ...holy

    ...graced

    ...blessed

Here are some people who lived (live) God's Song...

    ...Dorothy Day

    ...John Lewis

    ...Arthur Mirell

    ...Bishop Rene Valero

    ...Sister Rose Michael Hillary, O.P.

        ...Deidre Andrews

        ...Joe Clark

        ...Susan Schwemmer

        ...Roseann Maggio

        ...James Ragusano

*** Now you name some people... put your name there.

God sings to all "children of God". His song is woven into the ordinary fabric of each human being's life-story.

God's Song...
> ...embraces caretakers with solace and comfort
> ...is right there when one feels abandoned
> ...is reflected in our life lived well with Gospel values
> ...is a "servant song"

"Speak Lord, your servant is listening"
(1 Samuel 3:7-11)

True hearing comes from a heart of humble service. Every day (rain or shine) we have an opportunity to listen, grow, learn, and change, to stand steadfast to hear the Lord's song calling us forth to be his hands, feet, heart, and spirit.

God is with us on our labyrinth journey to the center of life where God dwells in each one of us. God sings in the center, but he especially sings at the edges and margins of life. God's simple song "ignites" a love that knows no bounds.

Would you say God's Song is...
...remarkable
...awesome
...inspiring
...comforting
...grace-filled
...challenging
...loving
...forgiving

***Add your description

—

31

God sings of the...

"Nobility" of living trust
"Grace" of being kind
"Blessing" of an open heart
"Presence" of Jesus' Love shared
"Gift" of sacrifice
"Treasure" of gratitude for the holy
"Companionship" at the foot of the cross

Each day take the theme of God's Song and...

...pray it
...live it
...embrace it
...listen to it
...share it
...become it

"Let your light shine" ...
(Matthew 5:14-16)

People of "nobility" are rich in living generous lives.
>   Annie Esposito
>   Vito DiBona

"Grace" empowers us to be extra loving to all people.
>   Deidre Andrews
>   Valerie Cherry

"Open Hearts" are truly a blessing.
>   Carol Hansen
>   Peg Franco.

"Presence" is the soil of holiness.
>   Arthur Mirell
>   Joe Clark

"Gift" is wrapped in human goodness.
>   Kelly Boger (niece)
>   Christine Lyons (niece)

"Treasure" is full of good memories never forgotten.
>   Bill Clark (nephew and godson)
>   Sister Marilyn Breen, O.P.

"Companionship" is knowing that God is there always!
>   Dr. James Lynch, M.D.
>   Joan Davenport

God's Song is about "People of God" ...
that's who we are!
>   Ralph Iskaros
>   Msgr. Steven Ferrari

God's sings of forgiveness from the heart that touches gently...

> ...anger
> ...hurt
> ...depression
> ...stress
> ...violence
> ...harshness

The song of forgiveness brings...

> ...peace
> ...hope
> ...self-control
> ...charity
> ...reconciliation
> ...kindness

Forgiveness is a "necessary" lyric to sing into one's daily life. It paves the way for justice and hope to be re-born time and time again. It is not always so easy to forgive. God shows us how to be merciful and loving. We forgive with God's Song of "grace" in our heart. Forgiveness renews our heart and the heart of the world. Forgiveness is a bold spiritual truth...it brings us closer to living God's Song.

"be kind to one another, tender-hearted and forgiving" ...
(Ephesians 4:32)

God's Song is not about...

> ...profit
> ...popularity
> ...power

It is a holy song about "humble" discipleship that...

> ...lets go of my way only
> ...is less self-centered but other-centered
> ...is a servant of peace

So often, we humans seem to be motivated by external praise, accolades etc. etc. (Now that can be fine, but there is a deeper and more spiritual way of being motivated...it is called God's way.)

The Lord's Song calls us forth...

> ...to serve in hidden places
> ...to sharing unconditional love
> ...to be merciful in words and deeds
> ...to be generous of time and talents
> ...to endure hardships by trusting him more

What motivates you?
How do you serve the Lord in hidden places?

How has God's Song of "unconditional" love
transformed your life?

Think of names you would give to God's
Song... and why?

Here are some I thought of...
>Valiant News
>Forever By My Side
>Good News for Everybody
>God's Heart-Beat
>Listen In the Silence
>Get Up and Walk with Faith
>Be My Grace for Today, Lord
>You Can Do It!
>I Hold Your Tears
>Smile ~~God Loves You

Choose one of my song titles or share one
of your own song titles.

Tell why...and what the song's title is saying to you.

Draw in the box a symbol for your song.

***my symbol is a heart on an
open hand.

Are God's Songs always easy to hear?

YES   _____

NO   _____

BOTH _____

Tell why.

God's Songs are full of...

    ...grace

    ...courage

    ...determination

    ...trust

    ...truth

    ...faith-lived

    ...forgiveness given~~no matter what

    ...sacrifice

    ...service

    ...suffering endured

    ...dedication

    ...extraordinary compassion

    ...holy silence

    ...heart peace

    ...humble prayer

What other blessings would you add to God's Song?

God's Songs sometimes evoke different thoughts…

> …a wake-up call
> …time for conversation
> …just rest
> …whispers of God
> …change your path
> …confronting vibes
> …surprise
> …holy   holy   holy
> …now what, Lord?
> …stay where you are

What are your different thoughts about what God is singing?

What is God singing to you today?

Have you ever sung God's Song...

    ...with an apron on

    ...with a prayer in your heart

    ...very carefully

    ...with lots of joy

    ...with friends

    ...at a concert

    ...in a food store on aisle 6

    ...waiting on line at the post office

    ...in a doctor's waiting room

    ...walking a doggie

    ...sitting in the last pew in church

    ...with lots of tears

Name some of your surprising places you have sung God's Song.

1.

2.

3.

4.

5.

Where is God?   Everywhere!
God is in the rain and in the sun of our days.

We all have fears …Jesus took on our human nature…he understands our fears, struggles and sufferings. When someone shares a fear…it is best to listen and to tell them…be not afraid to be afraid. God is right there holding your fear. He is helping each one of us to hold our own fear and learn from it…our fears can teach us to be very compassionate.

Here is a little tune I made up to deal with fears.

"To Be"

Be not afraid…
To share some good deeds…with everyone (sing twice)
Be not afraid…
To give respect and care…with everyone (sing twice)
Be not afraid…
To love and celebrate God's hope…with everyone
(sing twice)
Be not afraid…
To be a blessing of Christ's love …with everyone…
(sing twice)

"Do not fear, I will help you"
(Isaiah 41:10)

This is the song you and I can sing by...
> ...being kindness for one another
> ...by accepting one another
> ...by being humble of heart
> ...by being a faith-filled and loyal friend
> ...by tending to the wounds of a broken world
> with compassion
> ...by sowing peace wherever we go

God's Song is sung by your good words, deeds, and actions. Its lyrics are sung by the way you live and share your faith.

Who Sings God's Song?

Nature does as...
> ...birds chirp
> ...leaves wave
> ...rivers ripple
> ...flowers bloom
> ...rain thunders
> ...snow blankets

Humanity sings God's Song as...
> ...babies cry
> ...children play
> ...adolescence dance
> ...elders muse

Human hearts and spirits sing God's Song with...
> ...empathy and charity
> ...hope and peace
> ...patience and forgiveness
> ...acceptance and love
> ...respect and justice

How does your heart sing God's Song?

1.

2.

3.

A tune sticks in your head. It is catchy and life-giving.

    Name that tune.

    What is it full of?

    How do you live it?

    Where do you share it?

Some tunes we have do not serve us well anymore! Change that tune...perhaps it is a tune that has become too self-absorbed and needs to be refined or exchanged for a tune that is mindful of other people's needs.

The best way to get a tune up is to tune into the meaning of God's Songs. God's Songs are full of life. They can teach us how to share...

    ...faith in action

    ...love for one another

    ...hope in difficult times

    ...peace for everyone

To have a good singing voice, you will need...

    ...self-confidence and trust

    ...commitment and patience

    ...determination and discipline

    ...clarity and flexibility

You will find these qualities in Jesus' Gospel messages of...

> ...humility
>
> ...sincerity
>
> ...extra compassion
>
> ...honesty
>
> ...hope

... "singing and making melody to the Lord with your heart."
(Ephesians 5:19)

Heavenly choirs sing "Praise to God"

We earthen travelers can also sing praise to God. (Psalm 105:1-2) tells us to sing our daily praise to God and tell him how our daily work gives praise to God.

How do you praise God each day?

We all have some kind of trial to deal with in life. God is right there to lift up our spirits and to renew and refresh our ways. Praising can turn darkness into light. Praising is a restorative blessing. It helps us to become more receptive to receiving God's spiritual tune.

Praise is full of gratitude.

What are you grateful for?

1.

2.

3.

You praise by your song of...
   ...applauding
   ...acclaiming
   ...cheering
   ...inspiring
   ...thanking

Think of the words in…

Praise to the Lord
How Great Thou Art
My Savior, My God
Now Thank We All Our God
Sing Praise to God
Love Came Down
Amazing Grace
I Will Raise You Up
What a Friend We Have in Jesus
All That I Am

Hmmm….is it the tune or the meaning of the words that hold your heart? Maybe both.

What do you think the lyrics of these songs might be saying to our world community?

God's singing is…
…soft and tender
…healing and peace-filled
…unifying and respectful
…gentle and calming
…reverent and loving

God reminds us to be…
…kind and hopeful
…forgiving and loving
…compassionate and caring

What song or scripture quote sings to you of God's heart of love?

Where is God?   EVERYWHERE!
God's Song is in a...

...church   ...homeless shelter
...school   ...rehab center
...museum   ...library
...hospital   ...group home
...park   ...farm
...restaurant   ...subway station
...deli   ...gas station

Name some places you have heard God's Song.

It might be at the post office where the
post office clerk says to you...
"have a nice day".

God's Song is in your ordinary actions of being polite, kind and forgiving. The tune comes from your heart that shares God's goodness.

Name 4 places or events that you felt God's Song was being sung with wonderful kindness.

1.

2.

3.

4.

God sings about a Good Samaritan.
The song is about...

...loving one another
...befriending a stranger
...sacrificing your time
...being a holy presence
...sharing your heart

Name some "modern" day Good Samaritans.

1.
2.
3.

God creates songs to help us share our human hearts.

One of his songs is about a young boy sharing 5 loaves and 2 fish. God sings about when we share from an open heart, we can do more than we ever thought possible. "Everything is possible" God sings to us.
We can learn to multiply goodness.
We can learn to multiply happiness.

Generosity is not about an abundance of material things. It is about the heart's abundance of wanting to share the Lord's presence of love.

You might just say God's Song is "Pastoral" in...
    ...themes and meaning
    ...embracing and affirming
    ...compassionate and loving

As we listen and hum along in quiet contemplation, we start to learn how to let God's Song fill our everyday lives with the mystery of his unconditional love. Now we understand a bit better about the lyric that sings~~
"God is with us".

Imagine the whole world community singing a harmonious chant *"together"* with different…
    …gifts
    …talents
    …limitations
    …flaws

Don't just imagine … go out and be God's Song with your acceptance, patience, and caring concern for one another.

Singing God's words into life ~~ is a grace that brings about a renewal of spirit and a sense of meaning and purpose.

<u>Make Me a Channel</u>
<u>of Your Peace</u>

This song shows us the path to take where there is no hatred but a love that affirms, restores, and heals. This song calls us forth to be a peace-giver. It tells us to live with holy lyrics of joy that console and comfort, offer tender and compassionate love that is full of heart-peace.

God sings with tunes of deep forgiveness that bring us to places of...
>...better understanding
>...mercy and justice
>...redemption and hope

How are you an instrument of God's Song of Peace?

Some of God's song-words are repeated over and over...like a chant.

> Lord, have mercy (2X)
> Christ, have mercy (2X)
> Alleluia   Alleluia   Alleluia
> Amen   Amen   Amen

Why do you think we repeat these words?

What words of God Songs do you like to repeat?   Why?

How do you sing God's everyday words into practical acts of kindness, mercy, and justice?

What does God sing to you?   To everybody?

God-Songs share blessings for...
...the poor
...those who mourn
...the meek
...those who hunger
...those who are merciful
...the pure in heart
...peace-givers
...those who suffer persecution for justice's sake

We are all citizens of God's earth. God's Song tells us that by living the Beatitudes, we will have a sense of shared happiness and well-being. The Song of the Beatitudes tells us in beautiful tones that as a disciple of Jesus~~our song will be one of "blessedness".

Blessed are those...who love to sing God's Song.

God sings with the message of the Beatitudes about the freedom of...
...giving and receiving forgiveness
...being charitable and extra kind-hearted
...being a presence of comfort and encouragement
...sowing seeds of justice and hope

We too, can sing with God as we share the spirit of the Beatitudes by...
...loving others into life
...daring to be a courageous witness of Gospel values
...becoming the melody of a peace-giver in our words and actions
...comforting those in sorrow and distress

How do you sing God's Song of the Beatitudes?

What does it mean to sing with "gusto"?

You might think...
...enthusiasm
...enjoyment
...glee
...joyfully

Imagine yourself living the Gospel with "gusto"!
...feeding the hungry
...giving drink to the thirsty
...comforting a person who is sad
...visiting a homebound person

Perhaps the true meaning of "gusto" comes from a heart that loves simply and humbly as Jesus loves.

God's Song calls us to go beyond "being comfortable" in sharing our human heart. God's love knows no bounds.

Abba...mold us and fashion us
Here I Am...I will go Lord if you lead me
Make Me a Channel of Your Peace...let me share your
                                            love
Take Up Your Cross...and I follow Christ
The Servant Song...I will hold the Christ-light for you
Follow Me...and my spirit will be with you
Prayer of St. Francis...Lord, make me an instrument of
                            your peace

When we share love...we are singing God's Song.

Buy yourself a rose today....
and think of the words in the song
                The Rose

Just remember
in the winter
far beneath the bitter snows
lies the seed that with the sun's love
in the spring...becomes the rose

The wonderful song, <u>You Are Near</u>
        reminds us of God's promise.

      Yahweh, I know you are near
      standing always by my side
      you guard me from the foe
      and you lead me in ways everlasting

God speaks of needs in his songs...

...climate crisis	...mental health needs
...war-torn countries	...gun-safety needs
...poverty	...universal healthcare
...immigration	...education
...disability	...unemployment

     All these needs/crises are inter-related.
How do you and I, sing God's song of mercy, compassion, and justice not just in words and speeches but in genuine, humanitarian life-giving ways?

God sings of being at the margins of life...
      ...thy kingdom come on earth as it is in heaven.

"He has come to proclaim the good news to the poor,
to free captives, to restore the sight to the blind
and to set the oppressed free"
(Luke 4:18-19)

Jesus shows us that God's Song is merciful.
To sing God's Song of mercy one must understand...
      ...being humble of heart
      ...deeply committed to living Gospel values
      ...not be judgmental

God's Gospel Songs are...
   ...all embracing
   ...inclusive
   ...be-friending
   ...serving
   ...compassionate

When we sing God's Song of mercy, one is called forth to display a God-like heart by putting good effort into each day by caring about those in need and speaking with kind and uplifting words. In other words: clothe yourself with compassion, kindness, humility, gentleness, and patience. We do this so that the kingdom of God can be felt in every human heart.   (Colossians 3:12)

God walks among the people...
...not away from them
...not ignoring them
...not rejecting them

   "Love is patient..." (1 Corinthians 13:4)

How do we sing God's song into our daily actions that bring peace and solace to another human being?

   "As God forgives, you forgive..." (Ephesians 4:32)

When we sing or just listen to God's song~~he gives us opportunities to share his love in concrete, practical and ordinary ways.

You and I can be a healer…
…with kind words
…with a forgiving heart
…with a genuine, listening spirit

"…love your enemies (or those with rough edges) do good to them." (Luke 6:35-36)

Jesus spread joy…asking nothing in return. We too, are asked to spread acts of kindness. What holds us back?

If there is to be healing, hope and peace in our world,
we must see Christ in one another...

    ...neighbor

    ...family

    ...stranger

    ...community

    ...relationships

    ...friendship

We can be God's Song of love by...

    ...pardoning

    ...loving

    ...sharing goodness

    ...faith-lived with joy

    ...patience with self and others

    ...plenty of compassion

Be Inspired...To Love

What a promise the Lord gives to us...to be the eternal presence of loving concern. Our faith can remain steadfast in the midst of life's storms...prayer is a song that will remain an enduring tune of courage. Let us believe together...that the unconditional song of Jesus' loving concern will spark the struggles in our holy tunes so that they too become the heartbeat of peace and justice, mercy, and uncommon love for all people in the world.

God challenges us in very human ways to sow his love.
(Matthew 5:14-16)
Sometimes we do not feel like singing....
We wonder ... do we have the energy or will to do what God asks of us?

    ...repent
    ...forgive
    ...reconcile
    ...re-connect
    ...restore
    ...renew
    ...re-energize
    ...resurrect

Being wise is not about being a know it all...
it is about being holy and loving.

My special ed students were very wise and loving.

One day one of my students said, "Sister do you know why you forgive" ...I said why?
He told me... "you just forgive, then you feel better too."

Well I thought ... my student sure lives God's Song (and shows me how to do the same)

(Philippians 2:1-4)

Very often the example of others can inspire us to live lives of generosity of spirit...being selfless is the right key. You will find in surprising ways as you dare to live God's Song in wonderful, creative, and life-giving ways that it is more blessed to give than to receive. (Acts 20:35)

God's Song has many blessings to share with every human heart...

> ...empathy
> ...sympathy
> ...comfort
> ...consolation
> ...peacefulness
> ...calmness of spirit
> ...stillness
> ...serenity
> ...harmony

Imagine all your actions humming (1 Peter 3:8). The world would be filled with a unity of minds and hearts filled with fraternal love, tender hearts, and humble souls. Hum God's Song in your prayers.

"I was a stranger...and you welcomed me"
(Matthew 25:35-40)

As we join in singing with God about being a good
...neighbor
...brother
...sister
...friend

We learn to rejoice with those who rejoice and weep with those who weep. In other words, our tunes will sing in the dark and the light of each other's life.

What does the song of being with and for one another mean to you.? How do you live this song?

God's Song shows us a marvelous pathway filled with glorious lights where we can refocus our thoughts, actions, and good deeds. This glorious pathway also helps us to refocus our mistakes and harboring of negative thoughts.

What lights has God given you to put into your song?
1.

2.

3.

God's Song fills us with a life-giving melody of many colors filled with...
...hope and renewal
...redemption and resurrection
...simplicity and better understanding

The Lord gives us each day our daily bread (graces) to shape us in his image so that we can sing his humble and sacred life-changing message of peace that can be re-born in each one of us by radiating the light of Christ's love every day in ordinary and wonderful extra-ordinary ways.

Christ Be Our Light...
shine in our hearts, shine through
the darkness
Christ Be Our Light...
shine with your choir singing today

This is Church...
> ...no wall
> ...no roof
> ...people singing with one another

This is Church...
> ...signs of Hope
> ...boundless tunes of compassion
> ...forgiveness with a heart tune

This is Church...
> ...living your sacred prayer
> ...sacrificing your time
> ...sharing your melody of kindness with someone in need

This is Church...
> ...people in compassionate choirs
> ...people sharing comfort
> ...people living their faith joyously

This is Church...
> ...when we see Christ's love in everyone
> ...when we share God's Song in a variety of tunes
> ...when we praise with holy, heart songs

This is Church...Sing with all your heart

**This is Church...It is God's Song
and how you and I live it.**

God's Love Song is Eternal and so we sing...

...Carry Us Lord
...Embrace Us Lord
...Touch Our Hearts Lord
...Lead Us Lord
...Be With Us Lord
...Cherish Us Lord
...Teach Us Lord
...Lift Us Up Lord

May your love song, Lord, enkindle within our hearts, minds, and souls~~a shining example and reflection of living your love song into our daily life encounters.

All That We Have (Gary Ault)

All that we have and all that we offer
Comes from a heart both frightened and free
Take what we bring now and give what we need
All done in his name

 **Sing or hum this chorus 2 times
Then sit quietly in prayer.
Close your eyes and listen
to God singing to you.

Draw a Heart that sings with compassion.

Write your own chorus in the box under the heart

God's Song connects generations.

His song calls all ages to be....
…holy
…humble of heart.
…peace-givers
…radiant lights of his love
…Jesus' love here on earth

No one is left out of being called
    to sing God's Song "TOGETHER"
Awaken Lord in each one of us the beautiful and inspiring lyrics of your love song so that each one of us can be transformed into a melody of verses lived well that praise the Lord in all our words, deeds, and actions …for your glory, Lord.

Have you ever said…   "God, where are you?"

I am sure we all have said this at some time in our life…we just could not seem to hear God's Song. It might have taken lots of prayer, support and even a journey into healing and hope.

God is always there…even in the darkest of life's encounters…
        …loss
        …tragedy
        …grief so deep
        …depression
        …despair
        …addiction
        …fear
        …violence   *God sings forever!*

PUTTING ON THE YOKE OF LOVE

Come to the God within, you who are tired and weary,
you who are overwhelmed and overburdened.
Here you will find rest, here you will be refreshed.
Let yourself be soothed and nurtured by the mothering
of God.
Let yourself go, release the tension of the day and the
stress that overcomes you.
Close your eyes and be in the moment.
Receive the grace that comes.
You work so hard, you carry great responsibility, and
you are weighed down with the problems of the
world.
You are bent over with the heaviness of life.
Come to the God within.
Here you will unload all that you have taken upon
yourself; here you will shoulder the yoke of love.
Come to the God within, not so that God can help,
but that you can help God.
Release your hold on the reins of control, and
surrender to the yoke of love.
Here you do not work alone, but with God who also
wears the yoke.
Release your conception of a God of power whose
mighty hand will set things right.
Learn from God the ways of love.
Let yourself be gentle. Nothing good comes through
force.

———

Let yourself be humble. Your strength lies in your
 truthfulness with self.
Listen to the rhythm of God's heart.
The anxious, rapid beating of your heart gives way
 to the slow, steady, strong, and loving pulsation of
 God.

Come to the God within and you will find rest for
your soul, for with God the yoke of love is easy and
the burden of life is light.

> (This prayer is from the book Heart Peace
> by Adolfo Quezada…an author and friend)

As you read and reflect on these holy prayer words…you
will feel that God is sitting right next to you sharing his
God Song of love, peace, comfort, and hope.

COME TO THE GOD WITHIN

We are God's dwelling place.
May our lives be rooted in love.

 May grace and hope be ours
as we come to the God within.

May the yoke of love teach us
that God's Song dwells within.

Come within…God's love is full of light
His Song is one of Glory.

When in your life did you feel and believe that God's
Glory dwelled within you?

How did you respond?   (Remember…life is a journey)

What did this time in your life teach you about being
a dwelling place for God's love.

Heart-Peace is a song that always has love as its'
main theme.

"Let all that you do be done with love"
(1Corinthians 16:14)

"…and above all, put on love, faith, and hope~~
these three but the greatest of these is love"
(1 Corinthians 13:13)

"Greater love has none other than this, that someone
lay down one's life for a friend"
(John 15:13)

God's Song of love is sung with freedom.
His love is incomprehensible.
Divine love shines forever and ever.
God's love is wider than the sky
Deeper than the sea
Can light the darkest night…filling it with heart-peace.

Think of how we sometimes hold love back when…
   …hurt   …perplexed
   …disappointed   …suffering
   …annoyed   …abandoned

God's Song tells us something wonderful…
   …that his love will keep us
   …that his love sets us free
      to love~~no matter what!

The greatest song lyric we could share here on earth is
"full of trust" in the Lord. (Psalm 9:1)

God's Song trumpets with mercy and humility.
His song echoes in the words of the prophet Micah:

> *"This is what Yahweh asks of you:*
> *only this,*
> *to act justly*
> *to love tenderly*
> *and to walk*
> *humbly with your God"*
> (Micah 6:8)

God's Song anoints us with a mission...to be his love.

God sings at...

>...a "make a wish" foundation for children with cancer
>...a rally for safe gun laws
>...a concert to end violence

Do we dare sing with God...do we join the chorus of bringing peace to the oppressed and broken-hearted, to bind up the wounds of those experiencing injustices and longing to be included...do we dare to sing by the way we live God's Song of love for others?

When we join God's chorus of discipleship, our singing will be ...

...steadfast	...resilient
...loyal	...charitable
...trust-worthy	...loving
...hopeful	...prayerful

God's Song is in...

      ...today's troubles

      ...tomorrow's worries

      ...the future's unknown

God sings even when life has difficulties and hardships.

God sings with hope born anew. It is a song of wonderful "companionship" that...

...befriends

...beholds

...embraces

...empowers

    love to grow and resurrect again and again.

God's Songs come alive in Scripture. They are filled with...

...risk	...prudence
...daring	...justice
...bravery	...vigils
...inspiration	...resiliency
...peace	...sacrifice

God Songs sometimes arrive in...

...a gentle pause

...a ripple of thunder

...anguish unleashed

...carrying a cross

Very often one grows through life-tunes that weave hope in...

...struggle	...disability
...disappointment	...addiction
...hurt	...sorrow
...loss	...illness

There is a song by Marty Haugen entitled:
Love Beyond All Telling

There are two lines in this song that offer comfort and hope in times of trials and difficulties that make you feel that God's love is always there.

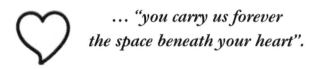 ... *"you carry us forever the space beneath your heart"*.

God's Song...
...knows what is possible
...gives birth to hope every day
...teaches us how to embrace diversity
...graces each one of us with perseverance
...is full of harmony and unity

God sings in every language~~ all have the same message...love beyond all telling.

God's Songs are not just words chanted; they are a way of life to be lived and celebrated. God sings deeply of unity not division. He sings of the way, the truth and the life of the spirit dwelling within each one of us.

God's Songs sing of the "human" experiences of...
...loneliness
...doubts
...sadness
...and love that heals

God's Songs sing with a hope of...

    ...making a good difference

    ...restoring peace

    ...climbing a mountain

    ...soaring like an eagle

    ...being a mustard seed of compassion

How do you sing these lyrics in your daily life encounters?

God's Song has some sad lyrics that do not get lost or skipped over. They are lyrics that cry out for...

    ...compassion   ...comfort

    ...healing   ...better understanding

    ...forgiveness   ...peace

The song of sadness is not sung to frighten or to depress us. God sings it to show us that all of humanity is...

    ...vulnerable

    ...in need of redemption

    ...given the grace of transformation

Think of a time in your life that someone helped you through a sadness or a difficulty.
You felt...

    ...consoled

    ...encouraged

    ...blessed

    ...healed

When have you been God's Song for another person in need? How did you feel being a sign of joy and hope? When you sing with God....is the tune touching, prophetic, inspiring, comforting, and courageous?

Dare to sing with all your heart.
Don't worry about the pitch being "just right"
On tune, off tune or a made-up tune~~God hears us.

"I will never leave or forsake you"
(Deuteronomy 31:6-8)

God's Songs help us to believe and remain steadfast.
We believe more by...
...becoming Gospel preachers in our words and deeds
...practice peace-giving every day in ordinary ways
...don't take life for granted
...see blessings even in the darkness
...dedicate yourself to kindness

All will not be perfect or even peaceful in the world...
We sing with a very human spirit...
    ...imperfect
    ...vulnerable
    ...weak
    ...limited

God uses our limitations...
"God chose the weak things of this world...."
(1 Corinthians 1:27)

God's Song is one of a deep and sacred justice that calls each one of us forth to be a singer of peace in every life-interruption.

God's Song tells us to…
    …risk
    …dare
    …be extra brave
    …inspire

How did Elie Wiesel survive being in a concentration camp and become more loving?

How did Nelson Mandela leave a prison after 27 years of solitary confinement and care more deeply about other people?

How did Dorothy Day promote charity toward people who were marginalized? She knew that feeling.

How does a blind man (James Palmaro) write poems about seeing God more deeply? His faith sees deeply for sure!

How does a mother who lost two children (one to suicide, one to murder) share a life of mercy and love? (Toni Bosco)

How does a man with the mental illness of schizophrenia live an extraordinary kind life even when he is made fun of? (Arthur Mirell)

How does a person suffering from injustices because of the color of their skin keep believing and trusting and working for peace?

How do people rebuild after a fire, a hurricane, tornado or devasting weather conditions that destroyed their homes and belongings and inner peace? Life has interruptions that pull at the very fibers of our being. Can we hear God's Song?

—

Will we dare to sing of hope....

...in the midst of destruction
...when sadness weighs us down
...when loss seems to deprive us of inner joy
...when peace seems so fragmented
...when limitations cause us laments
...when wounded spirits feel abandoned

Let us not be blinded by...
...selfishness
...harsh judgements
...lack of empathy
...violence
...hate
...disregard

                    a rainstorm can bring huge
                         wind gusts
                  people take to hunkering down
                        in a safe place
                   put lots of sandbags up to
                       ward off flooding

How does one handle emotional gusts of...
...negativity
...suffering
...human flaws
...limitations
...sadness

Perhaps we need to fine tune our spiritual life with...
...being positive
...being hopeful
...dealing with suffering better

God's Song does not always rhyme, but it has a good meaning. Its lyrics are usually simple and humble that blend well with unity, harmony, and peace. It does not have tricky lyrics but has simple, humble lyrics that relate to every person's life.

God sings to everyone...everywhere
"unconditionally"

All we need to do is to listen to God's tune of love and then share it wherever we go and with whomever we meet... be God's love in all your songs sung.

I think God is smiling as he sings his songs of...

Mercy	Love
Compassion	Joy
Forgiveness	Hope
Patience	Kindness

God smiles because he knows his songs are truly a good way to live, share and become God's word incarnate in the world. His songs are all about being selfless, open to diversity and a source of healing. God's Songs are revealed in all aspects of our human life, and very surprisingly in the interruptions in life that challenge the very core of our spirits.

<u>Heart-Peace</u> is a melody that finds peace by going through the pain, embracing your fears, acknowledging your sadness, touching suffering with your tears, gently feeling support and sharing it too. Heart-Peace knows God's "fine" tuning. It comes in moments of...

> ...deep sorrow consoled
> ...loss to be embraced gently
> ...suffering to wander through
> ...hardships to carry bravely
> ...questions to weep with
> ...heartaches to find meaning in

In some mysterious way this "fine" tuning beckons our suffering to become of service in compassionate ways. In the darkness of life, God's Song forever sings...

"I will always be with you..."

Though our hearts be pummeled by tragedy or sadness God's Song will always reverberate hope into our life journey.

God's Song is full of "blessings" that...

...soothe   ...unite
...comfort   ...heal
...mend   ...restore

God's Song is full of the "Salve of Love"

Ubi Caritas...God is Love (1 John 4:16)

How are you God's Love?

God's Songs call us to transformation during times of...
...grief and sadness
...anger and hurt
...violence and abuse
...war and destruction
...divorce and rejection
...death and dying
...hate and discord

One learns ever so slowly to adapt to life events
and adjust one's goals and accommodate to life
changes. By singing with God we can create...
...a new vision
...a new plan with God in it
...a renewed spirit
...an open heart

The new path is one of a "wisdom" song (Psalm 37:1-11)
Fix your heart on the promises of the Lord
and you will be secure.

God's Songs...
...lift us up through the shadow times of life
...carries us gently to a new space
...protects us during the thunderstorms in life
...understands our feelings of powerlessness

God's Song is about Divine Love's "forever" friendship.

God sings deeply of compassion and forgiveness. God's songs sing~~ "I love you with an everlasting heart". Can we dare to become more of God's love and be a person of deep faith and peace-giving ways.

When we sing with all our heart~~ we become one
heart and not be a people cut off from God's love

"seek the Lord all you humble of the earth"
(Zephaniah 2:3)

The graces of God's Songs are given to each one of us. Let us be courageous and dare to sing with one another.

Self-centeredness makes the world smaller.
A heart of love expands the world and
lets God's Love be the divine mystery
in our faith-life shared.
IMAGINE THAT!

How is God's divine mystery lived in your daily life?

1.

2.

3.

God shows us in his songs how to be truly...
...humble
...sincere
...valiant
...peaceful
...loving
...all-embracing

The grace of God's song comes wrapped in the...
...ordinary and extraordinary life events we each experience
...difficult and trying times
...moments of shared goodness
...times of letting go and getting up again and again

Listen to the "holy" silence in God's Song...
...it speaks of heart-peace
...it has strings of joy in it
...it offers us a comforting light
...it blesses quietly and humbly
...it calms the stresses of harshness in life
...it provides us with "sabbath" moments
...it helps us breathe in with restored hope
...it helps us step forward without fear
...it has a prayerful tune that opens our heart

When we listen in the "holy" silence, we will learn how to let God guide us, encourage us, and bless us with new and better ways of being for and with one another here on earth.

Sounds of Silence (Simon and Garfunkel)
Where do the prophets sing...and silence sing?

God's Song is one of...

...inclusion　　　...community

...respect　　　...peace

...solidarity　　　...celebration

How are you inclusive?

How can our world community be more respectful?

When was a time that you felt "community solidarity?

How do you celebrate God's Song in your daily encounters?

Is God's Song long or short?

Guess what...it can be one word.

Alleluia!

Say that word a few times and you will feel joyous

People who are deaf hear God's song in sign language

People who have special needs sing of trusting God

People who flee oppression and violence never stop
　　　dreaming of God's song.

People who are blind see God's song in faith.

You can always sing of God's Song...it has everlasting peace.

　　God's Song...

　　...shares tears of sorrow

　　...offers comfort and consolation

　　...touches disputes and arguments with better
　　　understanding

　　...embraces the struggle to forgive and be
　　　reconciled

　　...knows how human pain can devastate one's life

God shares lyrics of tranquility that lift up
a wounded spirit.
How can the lyric of "tranquility" change
the tone of suffering in our world?

How do you share "tranquility?

God's Song is in the midst of ...
    ...catastrophic storms
    ...deep losses
    ...divisions
    ...broken hearts
    ...wars of discord
    ...prejudice of any kind
    ...disagreements
    ...indifference

God's Song is about friendships...
    ...shared   ...celebrated
    ...appreciated   ...remembered fondly
    ...loved   ...prayed with

Singing (living) God's Song ...
    ...can come naturally
    ...takes some practice
    ...can be re-learned
    ...is so much fun
    ...has special meaning
    ...will inspire
    ...is challenging

Write your words to God's Song.

What tune do you sing?

How do you share your tune with others?

How is your tune life-giving?

God's Song is vibrant in nature. It is in…

> …the earth so green
> …trees and flowers
>> growing and blooming
> …seeds bursting forth
>> crops new with nourishment

God's Song is in creatures great and small…

…ants and lady bugs
…cats and dogs
…birds and racoons
…elephants and lambs
…goats and horses
…cattle and chipmunks
…fish and lions
and so many more

All sing in their own environment of Gods' harmony.

All that God created is good. It is filled with his message that all of life is inter-related. Nature teaches us to appreciate and be grateful. Sit quietly with nature and you will feel the tranquil message of co-existence that the creator shares with us and calls us to be for one another in life-giving and caring ways. Perhaps nature is whispering notes of peace and harmony, praise and welcoming into our hearts.

What does nature sing to you about the creator's love?
Draw something in nature that sings to you.

All creation praises the Lord...
     ...the little bird chirping in a bird feeder
     ...a fish swimming in a brook
     ...a flower in a vase of water
     ...a bee making honey
     ...a dog jumping for a treat
     ...a cat purring in its' bed
     ...a leaf changing color
     ...a tree with branches uplifted
     ...a ladybug on a porch
     ...the sun shining

     Add your nature praise...

1.

2.

3.

Praise the Lord~~
all creation sings
of the "goodness" of the Lord

What notes do you hear today?

God's Song is in a...
...heartbeat
...a tambourine
...a drum beat

    ...on a piano key
    ...a ukulele structing a note
    ...a violin string

...a child's laughter
...an elder's soft smile
...a cheerleader's exuberant joy

    ...a doctor's reassuring words
    ...in a stranger's offer to help
    ...a neighbor's kind act of shoveling the snow
        "gratis"

What notes do you share today?

BE EUCHARIST

God's Song is in...
...the breaking of bread
...at the table of companionship
...the new wineskins of life

Name some people who share the Song of the Eucharist
1.
2.
3.

Hmmm… think of how you describe God's Song in your daily life.

God's Song…
…is like a good recipe you can use over and over again
…a good novel~~you never want to end
…is the best advice column you could ever read
…is littered with graces galore for "daily" living
…is sprinkled with lots of sunlight
…is manifested in small and humble gestures
…is appreciated more than words could ever convey

Hmmm…God is ever-present.

God's Song…
…comes invited and uninvited
…is unassuming and always there
…comes from a heart…that rose "gloriously"

What would you draw to depict God's Song in your life right now……and what is God saying to you in the song?

***I would draw meeting a stranger on the street who asks me for prayers. God says to me~~ will you be my love today?

God's Song...

...can be a simple word or a sentence or two

...can be a repeated verse sung over and over

...can be a litany response that says ~~ I will live God's Song

...can be a prayer you made up for someone who is ill

God's Song is...

...in a friend visiting you after you moved

...being a "good" neighbor forever

...offering a kindness not asked for

...listening politely to something you do not agree about

...when someone simply says, "I care."

God's Song is for every...

    ...generation   ...creed

    ...race   ...gender

      ...nationality

God's Song...

...speaks of universal love

...gives meaning and purpose to all of life

...does not have to be memorized~~just believe it

...releases tensions

...never rejects or ignores human suffering

...is an instrument of peace

The lyrics of God's Song are for all humanity...

...helps us to reconnect to life better especially after a loss or hardship

...rejoices in choosing to be a light of goodness

...call us forth with compassion to address suffering

God's "holy" songs are...
...from the mountain tops to the valleys below
...calling us forth to commit our lives to serving others
...full of virtues to live and become better
...spiritual and corporal in good tunes shared

God's Song is there in our broken and wounded world.
It is there in broken hearts and wounded spirits of...
    ...gun violence
    ...domestic violence survivors
    ...survivors of abuse/violence
    ...divorce/separation
    ...survivors of suicide
    ...victims of murder
    ...in any disabled condition
    ...wounded warriors (veterans of war)
    ...mental health issues
    ...people suffering PTSD
    ...loss of a child
    ...addiction

God's Song embraces what is so difficult.
His Song is one of "holy" presence.
The Lord's presence is full of "graced" peace.
God's Song is a gracious gesture of Divine Love

God's Song teaches us how to live spiritually-centered lives. God 's Song is a tune we never forget. He has imprinted it in our souls that hold divine love.

*Think of a time in your life...God's tune spoke deeply to you.

God's Songs season life with...
...hope and joy
...compassion and empathy
...encouragement and forgiveness
...friendship and companionship
...words of healing and kindness
...acts of justice and mercy
...sincerity and hospitality
...gratitude and appreciation

What is your tune that season's life for the better?

God's Songs sing of "promises" ...
...where friendship understands better
...where one can translate misunderstanding
   into believing that life can hold differences with
   respect
...where distractions need not destroy our peace
...where "servanthood" is seen as a positive way of
   sharing God's love
...where "stewardship" is responsible and life-giving
   for all in community
...where we sing together of finding God in all seasons
   of life
...where trust is shared in unison with all

What other "promises" can you add that
you feel God is singing to our
world~~and to every individual heart.

What "promise" means a lot to you?
How do you live that "promise"?

Being human, we have common tunes ...
...joy and grief
...happiness and sadness
...struggles and resurrections
...loss and acceptance
...perseverance and feeling down
...success and failure

God sings to us...no matter how we are feeling or what disruption comes into life that is more challenging than we ever thought. God forever sings of his love for us.

God is sure there in the "in-between" moments of life...
...goodness and wrongdoing
...success and failure
...joy and despair
...justice and injustice

God's Song is ...
...precious
...steadfast
...loyal
...noble of soul
...graced
...spiritual

God's Song helps us to walk with our sorrows, worries and fears. He restores meaning to our helplessness. His Song teaches us about redemptive suffering and restorative justice. His Song is full of a light that refines our tunes to be an echo of God's melody of peace.

As God breathes his tune of peacefulness into our lives, we will be mysteriously transformed by life's intrusions. These seemingly challenging times become sacred resurrection spaces in our life journey.

God's tune of righteousness and justice show us that faithful resilience and truth telling bring about a better order and harmony for the world.

Nothing will be unbearable.
No frustration shall overwhelm us.
It will not always be easy.
Peace of Christ~~Pax Christi
(Romans 8:37-39)

No denying the difficulties in life
We take the path with the light
Nothing is ignored
We do not flee from life
Our loving creator sings to us...
    I am with you ...trust me.

What have "interruptions" taught you about life....
    and yourself?

What Gospel Song of God inspired you?
How have you sung God's Song to someone in need?

A PARABLE: THE LITTLE CHOIR BOY

The little choir boy was called "Sunny"
because of his happy personality and
pleasant disposition.
He always had a smile on his face.
Sunny was the youngest member of
the church
choir at "Heavenly Saints" Parish.
Being small of
stature at age 8, he had a special box he
stood on when he sang in church.
The other choir members enjoyed his company
and marveled at his wonderful, exceptional singing
voice.
Two more weeks and the parish choir would host
a special concert called "Live Your Faith" to raise
funds for people who were homeless. Sunny
practiced his songs for the concert. He was even
given a special song to sing "solo" at this special
concert. He knew all the words to the song by heart.
One day after school Sunny and his friends
were playing tag and he tripped and fell on
the ground. Sunny hit his face…it was all swollen.
It hurt to sing.

In two days the special concert was to be held in
the church. Sunny was not sure he would
be well enough
to sing at the concert. He felt very sad.

Sunny went for a walk in the park. He had tears in
his eyes. He met two men on a park bench who were
homeless. They asked him why he was so sad. He
told them about being asked to sing a solo in the
concert…and now he was not sure he could do it
because his voice hurt.
The men smiled and said, "you just BELIEVE that
God is there with you." Sunny smiled at their kindness.
As he walked away, he thought he heard them
humming the tune to his "solo" song. It made him
hum too…Sunny was not sad anymore.

The day of the concert Sunny was feeling
much better. The pastor told him that he had
invited some homeless men to come to the
concert to share their stories. The pastor said
that after the homeless men shared...Sunny
would step up on his box and sing his solo.

Sunny was beaming with joy.
That evening at the concert Sunny saw the
homeless men he had met in the park sitting
in the 1st row. They waved at him and gave
him a thumbs up! These were the homeless
men that told Sunny to "BELIEVE" when he
was sad thinking he would not be able to sing.

To his surprise when the pastor called the
homeless men to the stage...they stood
on either side of Sunny's box. After they
shared their stories of "BELIEVING" that
God would help them not to be afraid, they
looked at Sunny and started to hum his
solo song.

Sunny stepped up on his box and
took a deep breath and started to
sing without any pain...he felt great joy
as he sang. Everyone in the church put
their hands over their hearts and smiled
amidst tears of joy at seeing the little
choir boy singing with wonderful faith.

Sunny looked at the two homeless men
and said, "would you join me in singing my
solo song again ~~and they said Yes!

Everyone in church folded their hands in
prayer as Sunny and the two homeless men
(now friends) sang "HOW GREAT ARE YOU LORD"

As they were singing, Sunny noticed that there
were beautiful "heavenly lights" all around the
homeless men and Sunny too! He thought of
their kind, affirming words they had shared
with him about "BELIEVING" that he could sing.
(So can you!)

Everyone in the audience joined
in singing.
Sunny smiled. Hmmm....no
wonder he thought
that this parish is called" Heavenly Saints".

After the concert was over everyone was congratulating Sunny for singing so well. Sunny looked around to see where the homeless men were. They were at the front door of the church with the pastor and the choir director…they signed up to be members of the church choir. They would be standing on either side of Sunny standing on his box.

That evening as Sunny was saying his night prayers he prayed that all people would "BELIEVE" that God's love is full of life-giving songs and that we all can sing them by how we live our faith.

As you reflect on this Parable of a little choir boy named Sunny, I hope you reflect on how your faith shines hope and joy into your life and the lives of others and sometimes in unassuming ways.

Name some times you have felt God shining his love into your life.

What does "BELIEIVING" mean to you?

How do we help others to BELIEVE?

What would you call that box that Sunny stood on?

Why were their heavenly lights around Sunny and the homeless men as they sang...
HOW GREAT ARE YOU LORD

Now hum that song...and see how happy you are when you
"BELIEVE"
that when you sing God's Song   you become his love.

I Believe…
For every drop of rain that falls,
A flower grows…
I believe that somewhere in the darkest night,
A candle glows…
I believe for everyone who goes astray,
Someone will come to show the way,
I believe, I believe.
I believe, above the storm the smallest prayer
Will still be heard…
I believe. That someone in the great somewhere,
Hears every word
Everytime I hear a newborn baby cry,
Or touch a leaf, or see the sky,
Then I know why, I believe…

(hum this song…Perry Como use to sing it on his show)

Believing is a wonderful song to
sing…it is filled
with God's love. It is our
faith-lived.

SING OUT LOUD, SING OUT STRONG

I know what language you speak
You might say how can that be?
Well, it's the universal language,
      the one we all speak
Regardless of time or place, it's music
Music is magical, mystical, miraculous
It transcends boundaries and borders
      and diminishes our differences
It connects us
The very first sounds a child makes
      are more musical than verbal
A baby sings before it talks,
      makes dance moves before it walks
Immerse yourself in music
Move to the melody
Hear the harmony
Listen to the lyrics
Revel in the rhythm
Keep in time to its' tempo
Be inspired by its' instrumentation
Raise your voice to lift your spirits
So as the song says~~
      "Sing Out Loud, Sing Out Strong"
      "And don't think you are not enough~~you are
      And make it last your whole life long"
And when you sing or play music
      together, our hearts begin to beat~~as one.

(James Palmaro, a gifted poet with heart words written in prose.
He himself, is disabled with blindness and sees the world through
his faith-lived with great love.)

105

God's Song is:

...majestic	...sincere	...inspiring
...royal	...genuine	...full of goodness
...noble	...loving	...humanitarian
...true	...holy	...peace-filled
...supreme	...fantastic	...calming
...comforting	...soothing	...awesome
...marvelous	...joyous	...tender
...whispered	...healing	...kind

Now think of someone singing or how you sing God's Songs with a few of these feelings.

It is 19 years ago that I had an unwanted interruption come into my life. I was on my way home from giving a special retreat to eight graders at a school in Brooklyn. They would be graduating in three months. I had a wonderful day. I remember how they sang the songs I had in the prayer service. A boy who helped me put my things in my car said: "Sister, thank you for coming and get home safe." His words were like a song in my heart. I was hit by a 120-ton runaway locomotive twelve minutes after I left the school to go home. For a year I was in a hospital and had numerous surgeries, then to a few rehabilitation places and finally to arrive home to continue my healing. To this day I must take good care walking as I have been left with a limp and chronic pain.

I know through those long days and nights of recovery I kept praying a tune to God asking him to watch over me. Lord, I prayed, please give me the courage and faith I need to always have hope. I know God never left my side as he sent me fine helpers and aides and good friends who shared their tunes of hope, compassion, and deep caring with me. They were God's Song of love for me.

People of Faith...
look to God's Song of Courage for strength
(Psalm 23:4)
(1 Corinthians 2:3)
(Romans 8:26)
(Deuteronomy 31:6)
(Psalm 31:24)

People of Peace...
look to God's Song of living Peace
(2 Corinthians 13:11)
(Philippians 4:6-7)
(Colossians 3:15)
(John 14:27)
(Matthew 5:9-19)

People of Compassion...
look to God's Song of sharing comfort
(Psalm 86:15)
(Colossians 3:12)
(Isaiah 49:10)
(Isaiah 63:7)
(Matthew 9:35-38)

People of Joy....
look to God's Song of spreading happiness
(Psalm 47:1)
(Proverbs 15:23)
(Psalm 30:5)
(Philippians 4:4)
(Romans 15:13)

People of Love...
look to God's Song to sharing God's love
(1 Corinthians 13:4-8)
(Matthew 5:43-48)
(John 15:12-13)
(Philippians 2:3)
(Proverbs 17:17)

People of Hope...
look to God's Song to being a witness
(Jeremiah 29:11)
(Colossians 1:27)
(Isaiah 40:31)
(Psalm 8:18)
(Romans 5:5)

What scripture passage did you choose and why?

Read Scripture as a prayer being sung in your heart.
It has a message to sing~~

Tunes and melodies
Verse with meanings
Repeated over and over
People listening
Gather in prayer
Sung with faithfulness
Celebrated with joy
Comforted by holiness
Lived with heart-peace
Chanted with inspiration
In concert with God
Become one voice
   ...the voice of love.

Take a few thoughts from above and
write a prayer.
Let it become your song.

PRAYER:

God's Song~~Reflection Page

1. What does God's Song sing to you?

2. How do you live God's Song?

3. Was there a time in your life that God's Song consoled or comforted you?

4. What would some lines be that you hear in God's Song?

5. What Song or words make you feel that God is speaking to you?

6. How do you share God's Song?

7. What do you think helps to make God's Song a peace-filled harmony?

 (I asked some people to answer these questions put in this book. You might read their reflections on the next few pages.)

Father Mike Tedone of the Brooklyn Diocese says that the song God Is in This Story sung by Katy Nichole reminds him that God is with him and all people. Father Mike sings God's Song by the way he reaches out to everyone especially those who are struggling or searching for peace. Father heard a song on his car radio about brokenness and was inspired to give a sermon on that theme. Father Mike felt if he wrote some words for a song, it would tell people that God loved them in the good and difficult times of their life and that with his grace, they would be God's hands of discipleship... and they would make a difference in the world. Father Mike believes that the Holy Spirit fills God's Song with a peace-filled harmony. Father Mike sure lives the spirit of God's Song.

Those who wish
to sing
always find
a song.

Joe Clark, my brother from New Jersey, shared that God sings to everybody in good times and difficult times. Joe's inner peace hears God's words of compassion, and he tries his best to live them. Joe feels his family (parents, siblings, wife, children, and friends) have shared their songs of God and he has tried to listen better to become his truer inner self. Joe would write some lines for a song that shared about loving your neighbor, loving yourself and loving as God loves with an everlasting love. He believes that the Act of Contrition is a prayer-song telling God that you love him. Joe loves his grandsons...he feels time spent with them is God's time of love. He believes that the harmony of God's Song will only be felt when all people share the peace that God gave to each one of us...Joe sure does that.

The Word of God
is love
His Song has
your love
in it

Kathy Tully, a high school friend, wrote that God's Song tells her to be strong and believe that God is always with her. Kathy lives one day at a time. She did this with great love when her husband was very ill. God's Song comforted her and gave her the grace to accept help. Because of God's Song of Grace, Kathy in return helped and supported others through difficult times. Her favorite songs of Be Not Afraid and City of God strengthened her faith. Kathy shares that life will have many a challenge but with God's Song and our doing our best, trusting in his presence…we will find the peace that only the Lord can give. Kathy sure sings with heart-peace.

God's Song
helps us to see
things differently~~
to see with the gaze
of God's love

Joan Kovacs, my friend from Minnesota, says that God's Songs sing to her of peace, love, and charity. Joan stives to share these daily God-tunes into all her relationships. Joan said there were many times in her life that God was there inspiring and consoling her. She loves the Welcome Prayer by Father Thomas Keating~~

Welcome-Let Go of Emotions.

Let go of my desire for security...
welcome the Holy Spirit
Let go of my desire for approval...
welcome the Holy Spirit
Let go of my desire of control...
welcome the Holy Spirit
Let go of my desire to change situations
and persons and emotions...
welcome the Holy Spirit

Joan knows God is speaking to her when she trusts in the spirit-songs of God's love. When she shares God's Song by being a witness of God's peace and love...she feels the harmony of God's peace in her heart. Joan for sure has a piece of God's heart.

God's Song is
deep, ever so deep
It is a love-print
in our human hearts
Reminding us
that each tune we sing
is a welcoming echo...of God's love.

Jane Liello, a Prayer Chat friend from Kentucky, shares that God sings to us at every moment of every hour. That sure is Good News. Jane looks for the goodness in all that happens in life be it good, sad, or difficult. As with all families there were times of trials and illness to deal with which she accepted with God's graces. One of the lines Jane hears in God's song is that he says, "don't leave everything to me". That must be why Jane likes the song Here I Am Lord…God asks us to help him here on earth to be his love…she sure does that well. Jane has sewing and knitting talents…she gives back to God by giving to others (I was the recipient of beautiful yorkie placemats that Jane made.) She believes that peace and harmony will reign in our world when we all ask God…What tune do you ask of me?

God hears the voice
of those who trust.

Susan Schwemmer, a gem of a friend and volunteer assistant of Heart-to-Heart Ministry, shares that God sings he is my friend and loves me unconditionally. Susan lives God's Song by living the Gospel message of serving others with kindness. She knows that God has been with her during difficult times, and she has learned that God does not comfort us to be comfortable; he comforts us to be comforters. Her Song is: Close your eyes and think of me

> I will clear your anxious thoughts
> Call out to me when you are troubled
> I will hear you, see you, because you matter to me
> Wherever you are, I am, I will never leave you

(Make up your own tune to her words...I did...like a prayer) Susan says that you can share God's Song in simple and ordinary ways. Even a small smile can change a life. And you know what she says helps to make God's Song such a peace-filled harmony? It is when we all share compassion and empathy. Susan has a great smile!

Share your tune
It is full of God's Love
It is human,
wholesome and holy.
It has a great smile!

Renaldo Scott...tells us that God Sings of his presence even when we might feel alone. Renaldo tries to keep in mind that God is present even in the stressful times we all experience. He shares that God was there at one time when he struggled with his purpose in life. "I was not sure what career he was being called to. Business did not align with my moral compass. I left the job and felt somewhat despondent but kept searching for what I was meant to do. I ended up taking a teaching assignment which I thought would be temporary. From the first day of teaching, I loved it. Now looking back, I smile because God did it again! He was right there guiding me to this wonderful career. God's Song sung to me..."

Don't worry, I am right there with you.
Remember those times I was there, and you didn't
    have a clue.
I am not done with what I will do with your life yet.
Remain faithful with Me, and rest assured all
    your needs will be met.

Renaldo's favorite song is I Am the Bread of Life...He sure has been that for his students. "My students knew I was there for them just like God's love....it was a new mission for me to evangelize in my own way with God's Song in my heart. Living one's prayer is a wonderful way of re-connecting us to God and helping us to share the peace and harmony God sings to us."

Sing the Song
you were born to sing.

Rosalie Dougherty is a friend who celebrates 99 years of wisdom. Rosalie loves God's Song called ... Ave Maria. It reminds her of her two mothers (earthly and heavenly). Rosalie sings God's Song by doing good deeds for others. There were many times during her life that Rosalie felt the presence of God comforting her. Rosalie would write these words into a song that she hears God sharing with her...Love, friendship, happiness, and goodness. God's Songs all help Rosalie to trust that God is always there... when in doubt, she asks God to give her an answer to her prayer. Rosalie truly believes that when we each share our goodness with someone...a sense of peace and harmony is felt in human hearts.

Your song is
how you live
God's word of love...
with all your heart.

Mary Morris is a friend and an associate member of the Amityville Dominican Sisters. Mary says that God's Song sings to her of eternal love, faithfulness, forgiveness, and joy. In other words, God's Song is a wonderful love song. She lives God's Song with much hope that she will be graced by God with compassion, strength, and courage wherever and with whom God wants her to share it...family, friends, and all of creation. Mary said that many times she felt God's Song consoling her especially when she realized that she was the last living member of her original family...parents, siblings and husband were all now with God. But she was not alone. She was loved by God and blessed with a loving son and daughter-in-law, dear friends, and a beautiful association with the Dominican Sisters. Mary has a good life indeed full of Gods Songs saying:

> I love you.
> I am with you always
> Be not afraid
> Come all people of good will
> be and do good for each other.

Mary hears God speaking to her in the song "Hosea" by Gregory Norbert (come back to me with all your heart...) As she shares God's Song with others, it becomes a peace-filled harmony of all God's graces. Mary lives God's Songs bringing joy and hope everywhere she goes.

Sing everyday with your heart.
Sing of the goodness of God.

James Ragusano is a physical therapist who sings of God's healing song. James feels that God's Song sings to him of love and acceptance. James brings the message of Jesus' hope and healing to others through his work. He himself felt the comfort of God's Song when his mom passed away a few years ago. He loves to listen to a song about God being the sunshine of our life on the radio as he travels to each patient's house. James certainly brings a sense of peacefulness to all the people he cares about. He for sure is a lyric in God's Song of Peace.

God's Song gives to
each one of us
a "light" that will
forever shine.

Kathy Sheridan, an associate member of the Amityville Dominicans shares that God's Song is one of faith, hope and love. She strives to live her life by sharing these gifts. Kathy felt inspired and comforted by the love and kindness of her friends. Her song words would be ones of gratitude for the graces God so generously gives to each one of us. Kathy for sure shares God Song of love by the way she treats other people. She sees God's harmony in community... where each person is special and a reflection of God's love.

"for where your treasure is...
there also will your heart be."
(Matthew 6:2)

Father Thomas Ahern is a pastor of great compassion. God's Song sings to him a song of invitation, patience, and love. Father Tom lives God's song by living in the present moment. Father was inspired as a teenager to know God in a deeper way. Father hears in God's Song the words of St. Paul, *"love is patient, love is kind."* He also hears the blessings of the Beatitudes. Father feels God is speaking to him in the song Make Me a Channel Of Your Peace. Father Tom sure lives this song as he is a peace-giver like Jesus. He shares God's Song by celebrating the sacraments. Father Tom believes that working together as a compassionate church makes for peace and harmony in all hearts.

Peace is our gift
to each other.
Let's be this precious gift...
Let's be peace together.

Louise Mendenhall is a retired teacher who keeps teaching about goodness. God's Song sings to her about the sea and its' power, life, and gentleness and how those gentle waves of God's love soothe her and slow her down. Louise takes strength from the holy rhythm of God's Song. Louise believes God is there...always. Louise remembers a song from Mexico...

Madre~~a regresara turbrazos

Mother~~to return to your arms

Madre~~regresar y llorar in turbrazos

Mother~~return and cry in your arms

Like Jesus, Louise turns to his Mother and finds solace. Louise feels the song "Unforgettable" by Natalie Cole and Nat King Cole remind her that God is telling us that we are all "unforgettable" too. What helps to make God's Song a peace-filled harmony for Louise is when she tries to let go and let God, Blessed Mother take over~~Louise can feel them smiling.

Peace is an ocean of calmness
even amidst the waves of life.

Anne Esposito believes that God helps her to trust more. She puts God's Song at the center of her faith-life. Anne says that God has been there in all of life's ups and downs and deep losses. Anne loves the song Speak to a Girl by Faith Hill and Tim McGraw (bet that made you smile!). She shares God's Song by trying in ordinary and simple ways to shine her light by being and doing good all for the glory of God. Anne for sure is a beautiful light-note of God's Song in the world.

"Be devoted to one another in love..."
(Romans 12:10)

Sister Joan Klimski, O.P. shares that God's Song is a holy thread in her life that fills her being with the beauty of creation and the blessings of friendship. Joan lives God's Song in the whispers of divine love in the center of her being. Sister Joan prays Isaiah 49 and Psalm 138 trusting that the Lord's Song holds her close to God's heart. Joan enjoys her ministry of sharing faith with 5th graders and their parents. Joan is ever grateful for the holy lyrics of God's comfort and joy in her life. You might just say Sister Joan sings God's Song by how she shares her faith-life.

Faith has beautiful roots
in kind deeds ~~
Faith helps us to
share Jesus' love.

God's Songs inspire people to be better.
Some of these people still inspire us…

   …Oscar Romero

   …El Salvador Martyrs

   …St. Therese

   …St. Catherine of Siena

   …Dorothy Day

   …9-11 firemen saving others

   …hospice workers

   …volunteers at shelters

   …teachers

Add some more people you know who sing God's Song
and make the world a better place to live for everybody.

1.

2.

3.

4.

5.

Each one of us can be an echo of
God's Song by the way we
choose to live our faith

God's Song has Eternal Light in it. It is a song of Divine Love. These God-Songs touch our hearts especially when we feel...

...helpless
...sad
...scared
...anxious
...frightened
...lonely
...depressed
...unhappy

One single person can have these feelings, so can a whole nation. Each one of us can choose to sing alone or with others. It truly is how we embrace the meaning of God's Songs in our lives that we find better ways to be and better ways to live in harmony and peace with one another.

Debbie Boone sang the song...You Light Up My Life

You light up my life
You give me hope
To carry on
You light up my days
And fill my nights with song

We can take these lyrics and sing them thinking about how God's light is there in the day and night times of life.

Singing is praying twice.
Singing adds praise to God.

The word "sing" appears
in scripture over 400 times.
God loves to sing!

"Let the word of Christ dwell in you...
singing psalms and spiritual songs
with thankfulness in your heart."
(Colossians 3:16)

Songs very often sing of an emotion and elicit deep feelings from those who sing and listen.

Songs help us sing with renewed relationships~~ personal and communal. Many songs sing of peace-building.

Many Country Singers sing songs that are stories ~~
     like parables
The stories give life meaning.
These songs have not just words in them... but have melodies that...
     ...inspire
     ...challenge
     ...renew and energize
     ...teach us about life values

"...make melodies in your heart to the Lord."
(Ephesians 5:19)

Change my heart, O God
Make it ever true
Change my heart, O God
May I be like you.

Sometimes we hear a tune
  like <u>Change My Heart, O God</u>
  and as we sing it, we feel like
  God is saying "I am right there for you."

Some songs are called Ballads...
They too have a story like a parable.
Very often they have themes of peace,
  hope and faith that is lived well.

Some popular Ballads are...
...Stairway to Heaven
...Hey Jude
...Imagine
...Purple Rain

    These Ballads call us to live simply and be a
    source of peace for the world.

   Imagine...all the People
   Livin' life in Peace
    (from Ballad Song by John Lennon)

REFLECTIONS ON BOOK COVER

Look at the book cover. See the hearts on the tree. They are blooming with God's Song. See the branches reaching out. Look at the roots that are steadfast. See the heart in the heart. It is God's Song singing to your heart.

1. What are your feeling as you look at the cover?
2. What message is the tree singing to you?
3. How does God's Song hold your heart?
4. What name would you give to this tree?
5. How are you like this tree?

What prayer might you write using the book cover as the theme…God's Song…and How We Sing it

PRAYER:

A Concert is a public performance. This reminds me that when we live God's Song, we are in concert with him. When we live God's Song in our daily lives we become a concert of "holy" witnesses. TOGETHER...we can share more of God's tunes.

We are God's earthly choir of faith-filled witnesses...
...singing holy words
...chanting praise and love
...listening with a tune of compassion
...gathering in prayerful harmony
...sharing peace-filled lyrics
...singing with a humble spirit
...lifting each other up with melodies of God's love
...singing with each other on mountain tops and in valleys
...singing God's Song with those yearning for heart-peace
...harmonizing so all can sing God's Song together

"Sing to the Lord a new song..."
(Psalm 96:1-2)

God's Song...
Let it play fine, holy tunes into your life
...it gives meaning
...it challenges
...it inspires~~~
  ...justice to be born
  ...compassion to be embraced
  ...mercy to be sprinkled everywhere
  ...kindness to be our daily greeting

Live God's Song by...
...being Jesus' love
...being a sign of joy and hope
...inspiring others by sharing a caring heart
...sharing your life selflessly heart to heart

This is your
Song...it is full of
God's Love

God's Song is "unconditional" ...
...it has deep meaning
...it embraces all feelings
...it is everywhere and for everyone

God's Song is full of a light that brings a brightness of new life. It truly is a song of Hope. God's Song is full of "unexpected" graces.

A bird doesn't sing
because it
has an answer.
It sings because
it has a song

Life is a song...
Live your song well

EPILOGUE

I started to write this book thinking about some friends who told me that they cannot carry a musical tune. I thought of how they sure do carry God's tunes of compassion and love in their lives. God sings to each one of us with a special calling and mission of how we can be his song here on earth.

Everyone can sing God's Song...it is our efforts and how we choose to live God's message of *"loving one another..."* that becomes a beautiful melody of peace and joy.

God's Songs are proclaimed in his parables, miracles, and scripture quotes. His songs always sing about how a heart and spirit can be "blessed".

You and I can become the "holy" lyrics of God's Songs of...
...peace
...forgiveness
...compassion
...reconciliation
...transformation

We do this by the way we live and share our life by incarnating the Gospel message of joy and hope into our daily lives. What a blessing to believe that we all can sing God's Song by centering our lives in love.

ACKNOWLEDGEMENTS

I would like to thank all the people who shared their thoughts on how they sing God's Song in their daily lives. As you read their song reflections, you might find yourself humming your own tune of how you praise the Lord.

Thank you to my friend Susan Schwemmer, a gem of a volunteer to help me to get another book published with great dedication.

Many thanks to Ralph Iskaros who helps with symbols and a new holy card and flyers for the new books. <u>Ink-It Printers</u> continue (for over 25 years) to help to create cards and flyers for Heart-to-Heart Ministry. Once again, many thanks to James Palmaro who shared two poems for this book with such joy.

To all of you who read this book...I hope you are now singing with God's Song in your heart and spirit. Everyday get up... and be God's Song of love everywhere you go.

ABOUT THE AUTHOR

Sister Ave Clark, O.P. is an Amityville, New York Dominican Sister who coordinates Heart to Heart Ministry. Sister is a retreat presenter and a certified pastoral counselor. Sister Ave enjoys listening to spiritual songs and especially the message that they convey to each one of us…to live God's call by sharing our hearts and being messengers of God's Songs of peace, joy, and love.

Sister Ave believes that everyone can sing God's Song by becoming his love here on earth in ordinary and holy ways that are life-giving. Sister Ave hopes that you hum along as you reflect on how God's Song can be sung in your heart and with all your heart to make the world a better place for everyone to live.

"Love is patient...kind..."
(1 Corinthians 13:4)

OTHER BOOKS BY SISTER AVE CLARK, O.P.

<u>Lights in the Darkness…for Survivors of Abuse</u>

<u>Arthur: Thank You for Being Jesus' Love</u>

<u>Heart to Heart Parables: Sowing Seeds of Peace,
Hope, Faith, and Love</u>

<u>A Heart of Courage: The Ordinary and the
Extraordinary Becoming Holy</u>

<u>Be Inspired…To Love</u>

<u>ROSES…A Healing Journey for Survivors of
Abuse / Domestic Violence</u>

<u>Breakfast with Jesus</u> (co-author: Joe Clark)

<u>Peace and Compassion…Holy Threads</u>
(co-authors: Joe and Peggy Clark)

<u>A Light on an Angel Wing</u> (co-author: Paula Santoro)

Books are available on Amazon or by contacting
Sister Ave Clark, O.P.
Pearlbud7@aol.com   718-428-2471   www.h2h.nyc

Be God's Song...Together

God's Song...
...and How We Sing It

"…and with my song
I praise the Lord"…

(Psalm 28:7)

Made in the USA
Middletown, DE
08 April 2023